# Show and Tell,
# FLAT STANLEY!

# EGMONT

*We bring stories to life*

## Book Band: Orange

First published in Great Britain 2016
This Reading Ladder edition published 2016
by Egmont UK Limited
The Yellow Building, 1 Nicholas Road, London W11 4AN
Text and illustrations copyright © 2016 by the Trust u/w/o Richard C. Brown
a/k/a Jeff Brown f/b/o Duncan Brown
ISBN 978 1 4052 8255 0
www.egmont.co.uk
A CIP catalogue record for this title is available from the British Library.
Printed in Singapore
63261/1

**Series and book banding consultant: Nikki Gamble**

# Show and Tell, FLAT STANLEY!

Written by **Lori Haskins Houran**   Illustrations by **Jon Mitchell**

Based on the original character created by **Jeff Brown**

## Reading Ladder

4

Stanley Lambchop lived with his
mother, his father and his little brother,
Arthur.

Stanley was four feet tall, about a
foot wide and half an inch thick.
He had been flat ever since a
bulletin board fell on him.

Stanley's family was used to him
being flat.
They didn't think about it very much,
except when Mrs Lambchop needed
to clean behind the fridge.

Or when Mr Lambchop forgot his house key (which happened quite a bit).

To the Lambchops, Stanley was
perfectly normal.

That's why Stanley was surprised
when Arthur asked, 'Can I take you
to Show-and-Tell?'

Stanley frowned. 'You mean because
I'm . . .'

'. . . So good at wiggling your ears!'
said Arthur. 'Miss Plum really wants to
see it.'

'Oh!' said Stanley. 'OK, if Miss Plum
said so . . .'

Stanley felt his face turning pink. It
always turned pink when Miss Plum's
name came up.

Miss Plum was the prettiest teacher in the whole school.

'Thanks, Stanley!' said Arthur.

'No problem,' said Stanley. 'That's what brothers are for.'

Arthur smiled to himself. He knew the real reason Stanley was going to Show-and-Tell, but he didn't say a word.

At school, Arthur's classmates took turns at showing and telling.

Sophie showed her mouse, Squeaker.

'He just loves cheese!' she said.

Manny held up his grandpa's false teeth.

'My grandpa loves cheese, too,' he said.

Arthur introduced Stanley, who
wiggled his ears like crazy.
'My goodness!' said Miss Plum.

'Today I have something for Show-and-Tell, too,' Miss Plum added shyly.

She held out her left hand. A big ring sparkled on her finger.

16

'I'm getting married!' said Miss Plum.

Stanley felt his heart sink. Miss Plum?
Married?

The other children jumped up
and crowded around to look at
Miss Plum's ring.

18

'Let me see!' said Sophie.

She bumped into Manny.

Squeaker slipped out of her hands.

'Ouch!' said Manny. 'Watch it!'

He dropped his grandpa's teeth.

The false teeth bounced twice, then clamped on to Squeaker's tail!

'Wheeek!' squeaked Squeaker.
He started running.

'Oh, dear!' cried Miss Plum.

She reached out to grab Squeaker, and

her new ring flew off her finger!

To Stanley, the ring seemed to move in slow motion.

He watched it sail towards Squeaker and fall straight down over the mouse's head, where it landed like a sparkly collar around his neck.

Poor Squeaker squeaked again and ran even faster.

He zipped across the classroom, scampered up a bookcase, and vanished through a crack in the ceiling tile.

'My mouse!' cried Sophie.

'My grandpa's teeth!' cried Manny.

'MY RING!' cried Miss Plum.

Stanley stood up.

'I'll save you, Miss Plum! I . . . I mean,
I'll save your ring. And Squeaker. And
the teeth!'

Stanley raced to the spot where Squeaker had vanished.

'Arthur,' he said. 'That crack in the ceiling is like our window at home. Give me a boost!'

'On the count of three!' said Arthur.

'One. Two. THREE!'

With a grunt, Arthur pushed Stanley high over his head, just as he had done many times before. (Mr Lambchop really did forget his keys a lot.) Stanley slid through the crack!

33

'I see Squeaker!' Stanley yelled.

'Come here, boy! Come on!'

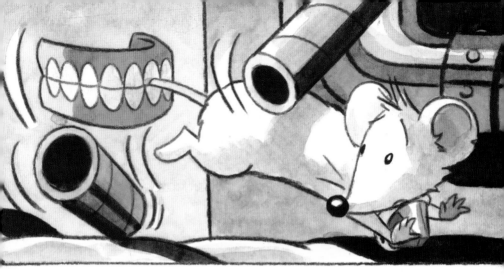

Below, the students heard crashing and thrashing as Stanley chased the mouse over their heads.

'Go, Stanley, go!' yelled Manny.

'It's . . . no . . . use,' Stanley said,
panting. 'He's . . . too . . . fast!'

Then Arthur thought of something.

'Sophie, where's Squeaker's cheese?'

'Right here!' she said.

Arthur grabbed a slice and flung it
through the crack.

'Stanley, try this!' he shouted.

The crashing stopped.

The thrashing stopped.

Then the class saw Stanley's arm poke
through the ceiling crack.
Squeaker sat in his hand, happily
nibbling the cheese.

Stanley's other arm poked out.
The false teeth and the ring dangled
from his fingers.

Last of all came Stanley himself,
stretching out of the crack like a
boy-sized strip of bubble gum.

'Oh, Stanley!' said Miss Plum, once he was safely on the ground. 'You're my hero!'

She gave Stanley a big hug.

Stanley felt his face turn pink.

Bright pink.

'What's wrong with Stanley?' asked
Sophie.

Arthur grinned.

'His face always turns pink when . . .'

Then Arthur stopped.

'When he's been wiggling his ears,'
he said.

'Thanks, Arthur,' whispered Stanley.

'No problem,' said Arthur. 'That's what brothers are for!'